FRED BEAR and FRIENDS

AT THE Doctor's

Copyright © ticktock Entertainment Ltd 2007

First published in Great Britain in 2007 by ticktock Media Ltd.,
Unit 2, Orchard Business Centre, North Farm Road,
Tunbridge Wells, Kent, TN2 3XF

author: Melanie Joyce
ticktock project editor: Julia Adams
ticktock project designer: Emma Randall
ticktock image co-ordinator: Lizzie Knowles

We would like to thank: Colin Beer, Tim Bones, Rebecca Clunes, James Powell, Dr. Naima Browne, Sue Stuart and the staff at Grosvenor Health Centre Tunbridge Wells,
Selby Chemist Uckfield High Street

ISBN 978 1 84696 505 0 pbk

Printed in China

Picture credits
t=top, b=bottom, c=centre, l=left, r=right, bg=background
All photography by Colin Beer of JL Allwork Photography except for the following: Shutterstock: 22-23c, 24.

Every effort has been made to trace the copyright holders, and we apologise in advance for any unintentional omissions.
We would be pleased to insert the appropriate acknowledgements in any subsequent edition of this publication.

Meet Fred Bear and Friends

Fred

Arthur

Betty

Jess

Also starring...

Dolly

4

Fred, Betty, Jess and Arthur are having breakfast.

Betty isn't feeling well. "I've got a tummy ache," she groans.

"Oh dear. We should get you to the doctor," says Fred.

Fred takes Betty to see Dr. Walsh in the health centre.

They have to wait to see her.

Fred and Betty go to sit down in the waiting room.

6

7

Fred and Betty find some fun toys to play with in the waiting room.

Dolly has come to the health centre, too.

She has come to see Dr. Singh. Dolly has got a sore throat.

After a few minutes, Betty's name comes up on a screen.

It is Fred and Betty's turn to see Dr. Walsh.

9

"Hello, Betty"

says Dr. Walsh.

Fred and Betty go in to Dr. Walsh's room and sit down.

"How can I help you?" asks Dr. Walsh.

"I have got a tummy ache," says Betty.

"Right," says Dr. Walsh, "I will take a look. Can you lie on the examination table?"

Dr. Walsh presses Betty's tummy, but it doesn't hurt.

"The tummy ache comes and goes," says Betty.

"That happens sometimes, Betty," says Dr. Walsh. "I will do a complete check-up to make sure everything else is healthy."

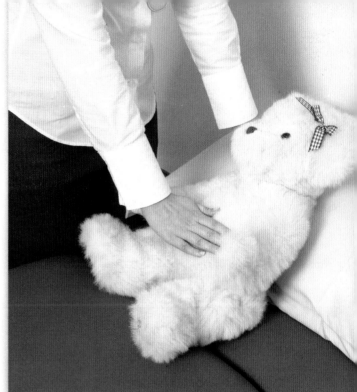

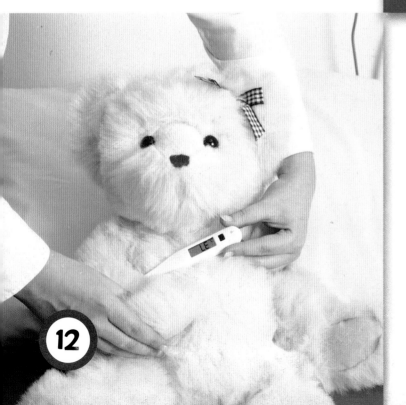

The doctor uses a thermometer to check Betty's temperature.

Then Dr. Walsh uses a stethoscope to listen to Betty's heatbeat.

'Thump, thump.'

goes Betty's heart.

13

"There is nothing to worry about," Dr. Walsh says. "Some medicine will take your tummy ache away. You should take one spoonful in the morning and one in the evening."

Dr. Walsh also tells Betty to stay in bed for the rest of the day and drink plenty of water.

Fred Bear says...
Medicine can help you get better.
Make sure you only take as much
as the doctor tells you to.

Dr. Walsh writes a prescription for Betty.

Betty has to take the prescription to the pharmacist.

The prescription is a note that tells the pharmacist what medicine Betty needs.

Fred and Betty say "Goodbye!" to Dr. Walsh.

Fred and Betty go to the pharmacy. Dolly is there, too. Betty and Dolly hand in their prescriptions.

The pharmacist hands Betty her medicine.

"Here is your medicine, Betty. Take only one teaspoon two times a day," says the pharmacist.

At home, Betty goes to bed to rest. She takes her medicine just as Dr. Walsh told her to.

Very soon her tummy feels better.

Her friends come to see her.

"Surprise!"

says Jess. "We have brought you a doctor's kit to play with."

Now Betty can be just like Dr. Walsh!

Staying healthy

This is a food chart. It tells you what types of food there are.
It also tells you how much you should eat of them in a day.

potatoes and grains

fruit and vegetables

Potatoes, and food made from grains like bread and pasta, are very healthy. Eat lots of these foods!

Eating lots of fresh fruit and vegetables is very good for you, too.

Foods with lots of sugar in them are not very good for you. You should not eat these things often.

milk, cheese and yoghurt

sweets

meat, fish and eggs

Fred and his friends also like staying fit. Here are some favourite games Fred's friends play.

Betty loves playing ball.
She is great at catching.

Dolly's favourite game is hopscotch.
She plays it in breaks at school.

What is your favourite game?

Foods from the chart

Look at the food chart. Do you know which types of food these foods belong to?

bacon

bread

apple

cheese